Nippers Beach Fun

Story by Annette Smith

Illustrations by Paul Könye

Contents

James and Ava

“It’s Beach Fun for the Nippers
this morning,” Ava said to James.
“You will like that!”

“I don’t want to go in any of the races,”
said James.

“Why not?” asked Ava.

“All my friends can run faster
than me,” said James.
“I’m always last.”

Ava sat down on the sand beside James.

"I don't always come first in races with my friends," said Ava, "but I still have fun."

James didn't look very happy.

"Try hard, James," said Ava, "and you could be a winner!"

Beach Flags Race

Lots of children had come down to the surf club.

The surf club captain called out to the children, "We are going to start now. The race for the beach flags will be first."

The Nippers in this race
ran over to the line.
James went over to the line, too.

They all lay down on the sand.
“Ready ... go!” shouted the captain.

The children jumped up,
and then they turned around
and ran to get the flags.

"Go, James! Go!" shouted Ava.

James ran as fast as he could.
But the other children
had picked up all the flags
by the time he got to them.

The Best Nipper

"The water race is next,"
called the captain. "Get ready, Nippers!
You have to run or swim
out to the markers in the water.
Then run back here to me."

“I’m not going in this race,” James said to Ava.

“Don’t give up, James,” said Ava. “Look! There’s your friend, Nico.”

"Come on, James! Hurry!" shouted Nico.
"The race is going to start."

But a wave hit Nico,
and his head went under the water.

James ran into the waves.

"I have got you, Nico," he said.
"Don't be scared."

James helped Nico back to the beach.

When the races were over, the captain said,
“James, you were the **best** Nipper
at our club, today.
You stayed with Nico and helped him.”